THE LEGACY *of* NOTHING

MANOJ PANDEY

WITH ILLUSTRATIONS FROM YUKO SHIMIZU

PAN

First published 2019 by Pan
an imprint of Pan Macmillan Publishing India Private Limited
707, Kailash Building
26, K. G. Marg, New Delhi – 110 001
www.panmacmillan.co.in

Pan Macmillan, 20 New Wharf Road, London N1 9RR
Basingstoke and Oxford
Associated companies throughout the world
www.panmacmillan.com

ISBN 978-93-86215-62-8

1 3 5 7 9 8 6 4 2

Designed by Ashis Panday
Printed and bound in India by Gopsons Papers Ltd.

Advance praise for *The Legacy of Nothing*

'A book for the twenty-first-century reader – pithy, groundbreaking, and thoroughly entertaining'

Prajwal Parajuly

'*The Legacy of Nothing* is an evocative collection of short stories, with prose as refined as poetry, modern as chat on Twitter. The unknown quirks of "ordinary" people, and their poignant struggles to exist, make Manoj's book a fascinating read'

Kabir Bedi

'Manoj's prose is lyrical and resonates with an acoustic that is as engaging as the imagery they evoke'

Bipul Chettri

'In *The Legacy of Nothing,* Manoj brings his unconventional literary approach to the fore with prose that is original and poignant'

Shashi Tharoor

'Manoj Pandey has devised a new literary genre that reflects the swift pace of our contemporary world. His vignettes beautifully capture the staccato rhythm and verbal sparsity of the raw lives of characters looking for love, success and fame, or simply struggling for survival'

Vanessa Guignery

THE LEGACY *of* NOTHING

to Prerna

ABOUT THE AUTHOR

MANOJ PANDEY is a writer and an illustrator based in New Delhi. His creative works have appeared in *Creative Review, Huffington Post, Litro, Indian Express*, University of Oklahoma's literary journal, *World Literature Today*, Wellington City Libraries, among others and have also been exhibited at Tate, London and Motherland, New Delhi. In 2014, he was named as one of the '200 Best Illustrators in the World' by *Lurzer's Archive*. His edited book of short fiction *Tales on Tweet* featuring stories from Salman Rushdie, Margaret Atwood, Shashi Tharoor, among others, was published in 2016.

His recent venture, an initiative to make literature accessible to the common man is slowly gaining acclaim far and wide. It is being termed as the 'World's Largest Public Library'.

He is also the India-representative of the New Prize in Literature, Sweden.

ABOUT THE ILLUSTRATOR

MANOJ PANDEY is a writer and an illustrator based in New Delhi. His creative works have appeared in *Creative Review*, *Huffington Post*, *Litro*, *Indian Express*, University of Oklahoma's literary journal, *World Literature Today*, Wellington City Libraries, among others and have also been exhibited at Tate, London and Motherland, New Delhi. In 2014, he was named as one of the 200 Best Illustrators in the World by Lürzers Archive. His edited book of short fiction *Tales by Timer* featuring stories from Salman Rushdie, Margaret Atwood, Shashi Tharoor, among others, was published in 2018.

His recent venture, an initiative to make literature accessible to the common man is slowly gaining acclaim far and wide. It is being termed as the World's Largest Public Library.

He is also the India representative of the Kenef Prize in Literature, Sweden.

YUKO SHIMIZU is a Japanese illustrator based in New York and instructor at the School of Visual Arts. *Newsweek* Japan had chosen Yuko as one of the '100 Japanese People the World Respects' in 2009. Her monograph, *Living with Yuko* (2016) has been steadily gathering critical acclaim since its release.

Her work can be prominently seen on Gap t-shirts, Pepsi cans, Visa billboards, Microsoft and Target ads, as well as on some of the book covers of Penguin, Scholastic, DC Comics, and on the pages of *New York Times*, *Time*, *Rolling Stone*, *New Yorker* and many other publications. She works at her studio in midtown Manhattan, and fulfills her passion of world travel by giving lectures and workshops around the world and in various cities in the US. She has not yet hit the mid-life crisis, probably because she became an artist.

The creative act requires not only freedom but also this assumption of freedom. If the creative artist worries if he will still be free tomorrow, then he will not be free today. If he is afraid of the consequences of his choice of subject or of his manner of treatment of it, then his choices will not be determined by his talent, but by fear. If we are not confident of our freedom, then we are not free.

—Salman Rushdie, *On Censorship*

CONTENTS

FOREWORD

In today's rapid and ever-changing world, technology has impacted the way we interact with and express ourselves to the world. From entertainment to food to political opinions and news, we have become accustomed to information in snippets, for easy consumption. Literature itself is undergoing a similar transition. Indeed, as someone who once read a book a day for a whole year, the current wave of insta-poetry, tiny tales, and Tumblr posts has introduced me to an interesting new dimension to storytelling and to engaging with one's audience.

Manoj Pandey is a product of this new age. He has carved a niche for himself, catering to those millennial, urban readers who spend more time in front of a screen than a sheet of paper. In The Legacy of Nothing, Manoj brings his unconventional literary approach to the fore with prose that is original and poignant. It is rich, deeply moving, and holds a reflective mirror to our society where people fall in love on the Internet, success is found on reality TV, and sensitive political issues are reduced to WhatsApp forwards that stoke tensions and inflame unrest.

Shashi Tharoor

OVERTURE

Some people get the acclaim.

Fame.
Success.
Or at least, the money.

Some remain *critical* in anonymity.

This collection is a documentation of such
anonymous souls,

Who, by choice or by fate, prevail
in the burrows of obscurity –

Often to *perish*.

A struggling musician, who is ready to ride on any cause for fame, including a minor rape victim.

A girl, who is in love with a man who makes her a part of a new age roleplay.

A phoney, who signs a book translation deal with the world's greatest author.

A story of Americanization that has a rippling effect on a girl in Delhi.

A Maoist from Nepal, who finds solace in a sip of Coca-Cola in Delhi.

A victim of identity politics, who is forced by fate to change his sex.

A town caught in identity crisis makes a hero out of a reality TV show contestant.

An online romance which climaxes into a reality that is nothing short of gallows humour.

A music teacher, from a reputed school, whose life begins and ends in a trash bin.

A boy, who takes his life for granted meets with an inconclusive result at a film subtitling firm.

All these anonymous people come together in this book – to tell their stories.

Decay

I was a regular there,
At Bob's place.

Friend. Confidant.
Rival.

He always kept me on my toes.
And I, him on his.

We were roommates in college.

From the worst to the best of times;
We revelled together.

From joints to smack to pills;
We indulged heroically – to the point of paranoia.

From girls to boys;
We *swung* equally well.

We were –
What they call, *thick pals*.

But that particular evening, began on a different note.
It wasn't going to be regular.

The usual, as we would say.

A special guest would be amongst us.
Bob had apprised me.

The vocalist of the band, Decay!

I reached early.

The guest hadn't arrived then.

Bob was preparing punches,
In a green bucket.

'One *hell* of a drinker he is!'
Bob informed me,
About the vocalist.

He called himself, Nick –
Which *wasn't* his real name.

Of course!

I ensconced myself on the couch,
In front of the TV.
Flitting channels endlessly.

Arvind Kejriwal was everywhere.

'The antithesis of the modern day Indian politician,'
That's how *Time* magazine described him.

He started as an aide of the reformist, Anna Hazare.
The pioneer of the great Indian anti-corruption
movement.

Just as I was ruminating on it . . .
A surly man with an unruly mane of hair walked in.

'Hello!' I said.
But he didn't acknowledge my greetings.

He lunged towards the kitchen.

As if he couldn't wait for his drink.

Inside, I could hear the loud *hellos*.
Bob seemed ecstatic to have him over.

'Must be some guy,' I presumed.
Resuming my news binge.

I cared less;
I seldom *am* star-struck.

Very soon, Bob and Nick began drinking;
In a room next to the living area.

Bob called it his study.
(But that was just one of his pretensions.)

It was, in reality, his wife's laundry space.

An anteroom in the bowels of their 3 BHK.

The space was stuffed with clothes
And a washing machine –
Old but still in service.

Bob couldn't afford such luxury –
He was just a part-time professor in LSR.

And an aspiring documentarist.

I joined them,
Casually.

I got curious.

They were discussing a music video.
For Decay.

Bob was giving Nick one idea after another.
And Nick was *conveniently* dissing all of them.

Bob, the banal.
Bob, the banal.
Bob, the banal.

Echoed in my head.

After an unproductive round of bandying,
They turned towards me.

Before they could ask,
I conveniently declined sharing ideas,
By saying, 'I am quite bad at it.'

And that, 'I'd be happy to learn a few things from them.'

I shouldn't have made the last statement.
Nick took it as an invitation to gloat,
Over his little glories.

This and that.

Small-time, clearly.
But quite remarkable in his eyes.

Things like –
5k hits on YouTube,
For a music video he did for Anna Hazare.

'We have to do something like this.
Ride on some cause,'
Is what Nick said.

It had worked for him earlier.

No words on ethics.
Or espousing a cause one feels for.
Or genuineness of any sort.

Just an objective view of causes
And figuring some way to use it –

For the benefit of Decay.
And his own.

Somehow
And in some way –
Gather fame.

'What plagues Delhi?
Let us think on that,'
He continued.

'Africans in Khirki.
Dalits somewhere.
Bihari workers.'

He went on.

'Think something new, guys!
Go crazy!'

What a shallow creature Nick was!

Incredible!
To the core.

Then Bob interjected.
He played a video.

It was a documentary.
By some British guy.

'Have you heard of the Magician's Colony?
Who are being evicted from their land
By the Delhi Municipal Corporation.'

'Who?'
I asked.

'The gypsies from Rajasthan.
They settled in the heart of the capital city, Delhi.
The magicians.
The puppeteers.
The street performers.

Whatever you call them.'

Such was the tone,
Of both of them.

Nick watched the documentary for a while,
Then said: 'No, not compelling enough.
Should be something new.'

'It should be topical, guys.
Think hard!'

I watched Nick blabber.

And gesticulate.
Just like an orangutan.

And Bob obstinately clung to every word of his.
As if the music video was going to be his big break.

From academia.
From ennui.

From the tedious theoretic life of a decaying old pedant.

Until Nick uttered: 'Infant rape.'

12 , 13

Inadequacy

It started with a picture,
On Facebook.

A tiny thumbnail,
On mobile screen.

Stunning looks,
Withdrawn eyes.

Sharp features.

Objective beauty.
(Not in the eyes of the beholder beauty.)

Absolute genius!
No explanations needed.

Dexterous,
Sublime,
Pitch-perfect in its sharpness.

What lured me the most?
Her utter inadequacy to be a useful thing.

Her updates were posters of vanity.
Her pictures pleading an otiose appeal.

I hit the 'send friend request' button.
And forgot about it.

Days of ennui passed.

Vacuous.

Until she accepted my request.
Thus, began my warped conquest of romance.

'Are you looking for a job?'
I asked her randomly on Facebook.

'Yes, I am,' she replied.

'I may have something for you.'
My response was post-haste.

As if to say,
I can't let this go.

'I'm currently vacationing.
I shall get in touch once I'm back,'
She replied.

'Sure,' I said, giving her my number.
She reciprocated.

Wow!
That was fast, I told myself.

At forty, this ought to be my lucky day.

For about a week, I restrained myself from dialling her number.
I didn't want to move *that* fast.

It was a lesson from Kate Blanchet in *Blue Jasmine*,
A Woody Allen-film.

Then, one night.

I called her up.

She said, 'hello.'
'Hey,' I replied.

'Sorry, it's a bit late but I'm in a situation.
I need a secretary urgently.'

'But you haven't seen my resume?'
She replied.

'Oh yes, I will.
Can you send it to me quickly?'

'Will do.'

'Cool.'
I ended it there.

Things moved fast.

She came over for an interview.
'I'm at the reception,'
She texted.

'Hang on.
Just wrapping up a meeting,'
I replied.

I didn't want to sound like I'd been waiting for her arrival –
All this *god-damned* while.

Frequently fixing my hair in the office washroom,

I counted to a thousand,
In my head,
As I scrolled down on Facebook.

'Okay,' I told myself,
'Act resigned.'

Holding my laptop, I went towards the reception.

She was there.

Fuck!
All so easy breezy
Like a tropical flower.

Imagine a bunch of Tiger lilies,
With a subtle scent of detachment.

Her gaze told me, 'Hello, fuck-head.'
I obliged with a lured look.

She just smiled.
And stood up like a lyrical bird.

I was in trouble.
I sensed it from that moment on.

To clarify,
She wasn't a typical bluestocking.
Or a desperate wannabe.

Her presence was feline and predatory;
I felt like a goat on a string.

Okay.
Enough of the paean.

I led her in,
To a large conference room.

And completed the ritual of exchanging the
preliminary pleasantries.
As if we were both meeting after long.

With phrases such as: 'I'm this and that.'

She didn't say a word.
She was quiet.
Crimping her lips to force an occasional smile.

I felt the coke of love melt inside me.

'So, show me your resume,'
I said.

An attempt to distract myself from where all this talk
was leading to, at least in my head.

Her resume was average.
Too liminal for her age and experience.

It had the potential of a twenty year old.
But not the maturity of a thirty-something woman.

Definitely, *not* the right candidate.

But, of course.

Did that *really* matter?

No.

Surely, not.

'Great, I'll get back to you shortly,'
I said.

I had to put up that act,
Despite being the shot-caller.

I waited.
Patiently.

Until she called me up after a week.

By then, I had already done all the paperwork.
And ensured that I would be the harbinger of good tidings to her.

'You're hired,'
I said.

She was happy.
It was beautiful.
I tripped on her Facebook for about an hour after that.

She was joining after two weeks.
And, poor me, I couldn't wait for a second more.

After about four days or so,
I rang her up.

'Hey!'

At first, I was wordless after that salutation.

I then told her if she could come for an hour to office.

'Urgent times,'
I lied.

'Some crisis.'

She complied without complaint.
At 8 p.m., she was at the reception again.

After the same, aforementioned drill, I went outside.

It was a black tee this time.
Jeans jacket and chinos.

Stunning as a star.

Flawless.

I didn't know what to say.
There was no urgency.

After a short awkward chat, I asked her to leave.
'The crisis has been resolved.
I'm sorry for the trouble.'

She said, 'It's fine.'
And she left.

I went nuts over her pictures on Facebook again;

After she left.

WTF.

Finally, when she joined, I was at ease;
Not having to depend anymore on Facebook.

She was my go-to-person for every project.

I could talk.
Joke.
Even rant.

And she would listen.

For hours on end.

I told her everything.

About men, music, meat even.

One day,
She spoke.
Opened up to me.

And it was poetry.
Unrehearsed.

Every sentence was a lyric.
Every word was bespoke; designed to fascinate me.

Again,
I affirm.

It was unrehearsed.

The magic of her eloquence was effusive, spontaneous.

Rimbaud with the felicity of Urdu.

Magical, it was.

A time came when . . .
We started discussing work less.
And life more.

Now, I listened.
And she spoke.

Every syllable had the sweet staccato of a piano key.
Very Eric Satie.

Gnossienne No 1.

One night, we were working late.
I was busy with a presentation.

She was waiting for me to complete it.

So she could proofread it.

Across the cubicles, *we discovered*, we were staring at each other.
She looked down when I didn't stop.

After a second, she texted.

It was an Urdu poem,

Of indescribable, indecipherable beauty.

Somewhere between Bolano's *Clara* and Rimbaud's *Ophelia*.

The feeling, the imagination, the moment –
Are quite simply –
Ineffable.

The night ended on that note.
She left for home.

Soon, she was dropping me home.

We hardly spoke.
We only listened to Bollywood classics on the car stereo.

I was a Bollywood virgin.
Raised on a staple diet of Grateful Dead, Zeppelin and Pearl Jam.

The fucking melodrama.
The muck.
The mush.

That Bollywood –
Which now had me in its thralls.

One evening, before I exited her car,
She asked for a hug.

We dissolved.

Again,
Ineffable.

Except for her fragrance,
Her warmth,
Her *never-let-me-go* embrace.

It was followed by the obvious;
A long kiss before we parted.

And then, the more obvious one.

Sex.
In hotels.

Until, I began getting psychotic.
I thought she was my medicine.
I felt I wouldn't need *meds* anymore.

But I was wrong.

Our visit to the hotel began turning into a scene right out of an asylum.

She waited on me.
Until I had had my sleep.

When I awoke, she served tea.
And biscuits.

Naked.

Then.

On one of our dates, I told her about my addiction.
To *medicines*.

How, *without it*, I can't tell day or night.
Fiction or reality.

Still.

She stayed with me.
She never asked questions.
Always listened to me.

She was all accommodating.

Until we exchanged our pasts.

I showed her my *wife's boyfriend's* texts.
She told me about her divorce at 26.

Not that any of it mattered.

Anymore.

Her revelations were an *open-heart* surgery.
Not a by-pass.

Open-heart.

My revelations were of the same nature, too.

The fact that my wife was a *witness* to all of this.
As I was to hers.

Amen.

Anonymous

Just as I powered my phone on,
WhatsApp notifications erupted one after the other.

A clamouring burst.

It was Raj.

I find it hard to describe him.
A friend. Or, an acquaintance.
Or, a well-wisher.

Maybe a spammer.

I don't know.

I just remember him as a man who texts me incessantly on Facebook.

So much so that I've put his window on silent.

We first spoke over a call.
He wanted to write a review of my book for a Nepali newspaper.

It was a book I didn't want to associate myself with.

I was trying hard to erase it.
Every online footprint.

I had gone to the extent of deactivating its promotional Facebook page.

But, hey!

Such is life.

He never wrote the review,
Despite interviewing me for about an hour.

Though I'm eternally grateful to him for that.

But now, he's back again.
In my life.

I'm dreading another review request.

I rang him up.
As he is in Delhi.

And it's considered impolite to not call a fellow Nepali.
Especially, when they're in strange lands.

'Hey!'
He says.
As always,
In glee.

I don't understand his optimism –
In life and in literature.

Despite all odds.

He is a teacher.
Unpublished writer.
Who still thinks, at fifty, that a pen can change the world.

Or at least, tweak it a little, for the better.

I have to give it to him,
Such grandiloquent hope,
Against all hopes.

He tells me he is in Delhi,
At the Sahitya Akademi.
The highest literary body in India.

'What for?'
I ask.

'Meeting some friends.
For my new publishing house.'
Then adds (quite pompously) 'I have a couple of other meetings, too.'

'Where do you stay?'
Raj asks me.

'South Delhi,'
I tell him.

Without being specific.

'How far is that from Lodhi?'
He goes on.

'About an hour,'
I say.

'Can we meet somewhere in between?'
Raj persists.

'Sure,'
I reply.

There is no way out with him.
Once he gets his mind to it.

He's a persuader,
Of the unusual kind.

I never reply to his Facebook messages.
And he never stops pinging.

That's us, in a crux.

But today.
If I don't meet him elsewhere,
He is bound to find my home.

He knows, from my tone of voice and my blatant disapproval of his opinion over the Net, that I'm about to give him an excuse.

So, he drops a bait on me.
'I have an appointment with Ms Joy –
The Booker winner.'

I take it.

Knowing that, he says:
'Why don't you come along with us?'

'Sure,' I say.
Without hesitation.

After all, it's an opportunity.
A thousand possibilities pop in my head.

But I answer back with a blasé okay.

'Okay,' he says.
'See you then.'

'3 p.m.
420, Jorbagh.'

'Sure,'
I say.
And I cut the call.

I'm at a studio for some job.
But I leave with an excuse.
And head home.

I need a bath.
A black shirt.
Blue trousers.

And a black pair of shoes.

In about an hour, I get ready.
All set to meet Ms Joy.

I get late on the way.
I fret over traffic.
And fear getting late.

Raj keeps texting me.

Surprising myself, I reply.
To all of them.

'Wow,'
He exclaims.

Perhaps, sarcastically.

But I just ignore it.

When I reach 420, Raj calls me up.
We try to find each other.
And eventually we meet.

Fun fact: we're meeting for the first time.

He's got a friend along.
Looks Nepalese.
From Nepal.

Without bothering for pleasantries, we start speaking.
As if we are the best of friends.

Are we?

I don't know.

He is always there when I need to rant.
Always online.
At all times.

Ready to respond to anything I say.

Anyhow.
We reach 420.
At first Raj says, 'first floor.'
We ring the bell.

Raj then looks into his WhatsApp,
'Oh no,' he exclaims.

'It's the second floor.'

As we head up, an elderly woman opens the door on the first floor.

I apologize.
Profusely.

We head up again.
We know from the inscriptions on Ms Joy's wall that it's her apartment.
It says:
'You can't be careful enough. Because you can't be careful enough.'

We all wait outside with bated breath.
It's Ms Joy after all.

The God of the Streets was the first serious book I ever read as a kid.
I still remember it having a permanent place beside the old telephone in my room.

It was from *that* era –
When telephones were a status symbol.

After about two rings, Ms Joy opened the door.
She is still a gorgeous person.
A few grey hair don't mar it, yet.
Her voice is as soft as in her interview with Salman Rushdie.
Which was many years ago.

When she *was* as gorgeous as she is today.

Big moment for all of us.
Me especially.

I have had a serious crush on her.
All my life.

She opens the door and welcomes us inside.
Her apartment opens into a kitchen.

Lovely, quiet place.

There is a brass plate on the table.

It says:
Please don't use mobile phones.
Please don't use laptops.
Please speak softly.

Or something to that effect.

I am too smitten to notice all of that.

She blurs everything.

We all settle around a table.

She offers us lemonade.
Then the conversation begins.
There are tons of manuscripts on the table.
The walls seem plastered with books.

'I'm sorry, I came without informing you.'
Raj apologizes to Ms Joy.

I'm like, WTF.

She is kind.
'No, that's fine,' she says.
A quiet smile plays on her lips.

As if afraid.

'So, you're from Himalayan Books?'

'Not me,' I say.
Turning towards Raj and his friend.

(I don't want to be a part of this scam.)

Raj and his friend introduce themselves as founders of the publishing house.

I feel queasy inside.

Because the conversation is getting complicated.

She is speaking about translations.
And Raj is talking about himself.

While his friend gifts her a packet of Darjeeling tea.
'Silver Tips from Makaibari,'
He says.
'So, you publish in Nepali?'
She is addressing Raj.

'Yes,' he replies.
'We translate.'

'Is it a reading society?'
She asks.

'Yes, ma'am.'
We have forty million Nepalese worldwide.

I don't know what to say.
Or how to get them on the same page.

'The politics of disseminating information has
changed,'
Ms Joy says.

'Yes, ma'am.
We have a Facebook page.'

After a point, she gives up,
And turns towards me.

'So, young man.
What do you do?'

'I do nothing,'
I reply.
'But I'm a big fan of yours.

And I stole this opportunity to meet you.'
'Thank you,' she says.
Handing over the contract to Raj.

Raj has no clue about contracts.
Or translations.
Or her work.

Oh my fucking god.

By now, Ms Joy is aware that Raj is a novice.
At fifty.
But she is too civil, too polite to say it to his face.

I fall in love with her.
All over again.

Her power.
Her grace.

That maturity;
In handling Raj.

In getting into a contract with him.
In giving the right to translate her work;

The fruit of ten long years.

To a stranger.
To a phoney.

To, anonymity.

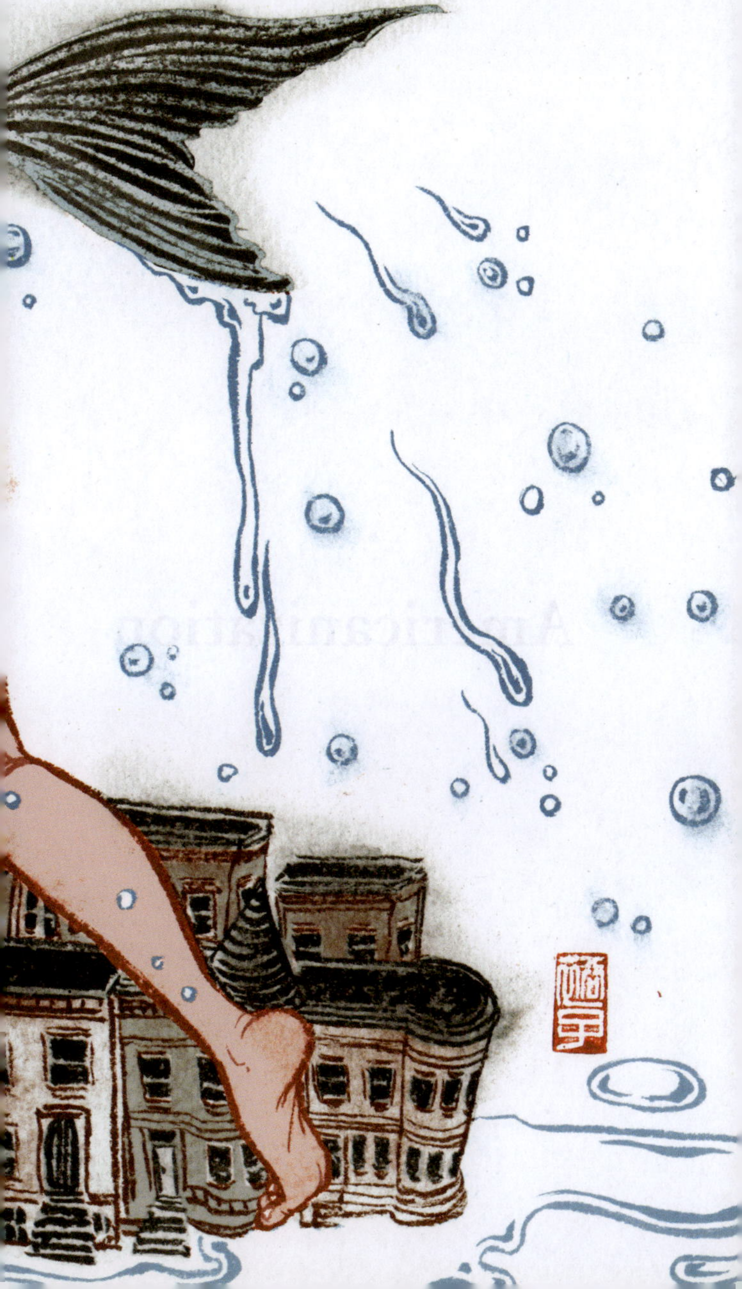

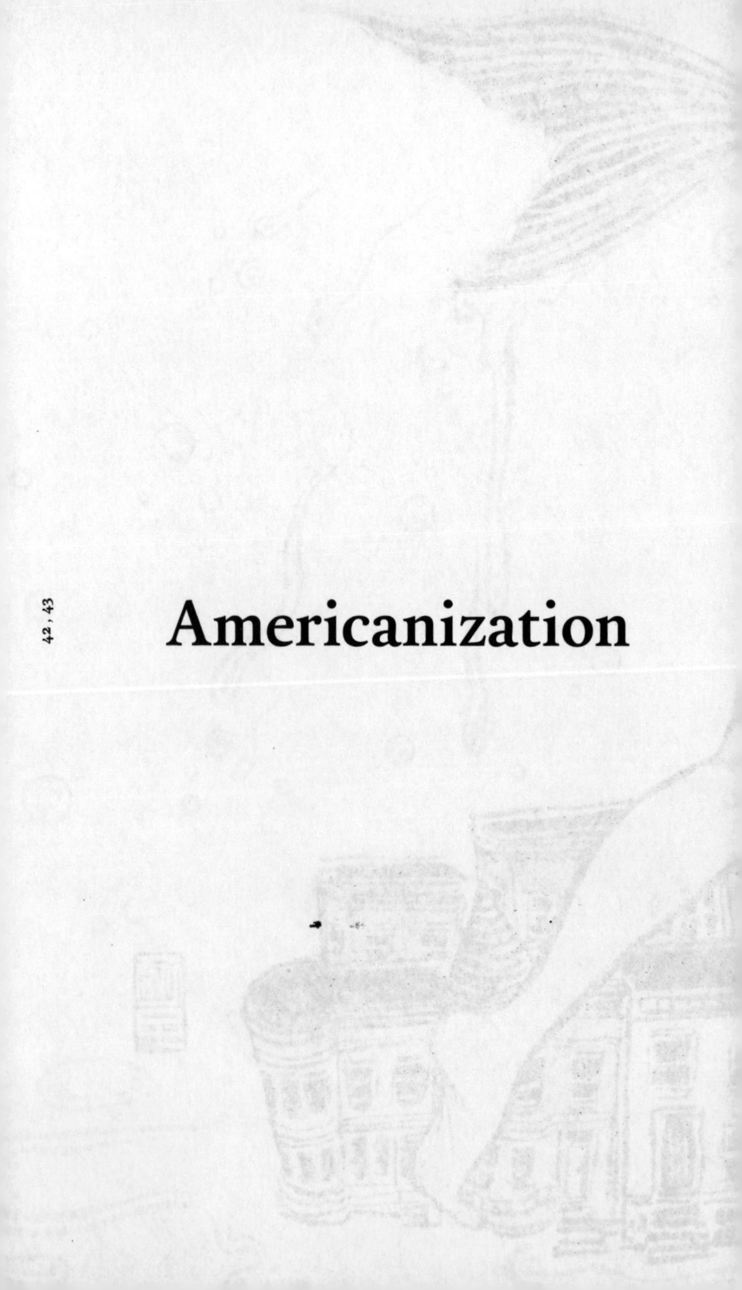

Americanization

3 p.m.

It was a lazy Sunday.
With nothing much to do.

Actually, that's not quite true.
Or accurate.

I was feeling drained.
And washed out.

From a routine doze.
Of schizophrenia pills.

White.
Yellow.
Of all colours.

And different mgs.

I'd recently come back to life,
From a psychotic episode.

Just a moment back,
I had watched *Cracked* by James Davies.

It was a revelatory video,
On YouTube.

On psychiatry.

A beautiful counter-view,
On why it's doing more harm than good.

About Robert Spitz.
From Princeton.

America.

About his empirical unscientific methods.
About how he is the champion behind Diagnostic
Systematic Manual.

The manual that sanctifies every psychiatric ailment.

About its gloriously wretched fakery.

Fuckery.
Wankery.

Its disreputable legality.

Before I could delve further,
Into a digression binge,
I got a call.

From Dorothy.
A former colleague.
And my protégé.

From Delhi.

I used to think she was gifted.
But now I have revised that opinion.

In an effort to forget her past,
She was creating an alternate reality –
Inside her head.

Overwriting her memory.

With constant thoughts.
With endless ideas.

Just to seek peace.
Each moment.

From hell.

From her dad.

A repressed, depraved IAS officer.

It began early on.
When she was only eight.

The kisses.
Tight hugs.
Firm hands.

The touch.

Dorothy had survived –
9 attempts to die.

Each time,
To be saved by her dad.

For him to resume the act,
As soon as she recovered
And was well again.

Rosy by the cheeks.

She hated *home*.

The sacrilegious domestic culture.

Hell.

After college, she *had* to move out.

It was the only way;
Away from the *monster*.

Away from all *of that*.
Unspeakable horror.

And from *his* incomprehensible *love*.

She was on pills now.
Like me.

Only in her case.
It was *SDPD*.

Self-destructive personality disorder.

Listed in the *DSM*
By Robert Spitz.

50, 51

Enjoy Coca-Cola

Circa 2008.

The *war* was over.
The king was dead.

The Maoists in Nepal had assumed power.
The *kingdom* had become a republic.

History had been erased;
To be written all over again.

In Delhi . . .

Maya had just arrived.
An eighteen-year-old from Nepal,
Who fled from her village,
Ravaged by rebels.

She had been one, too,
Long ago.

A foot soldier.

Who knew everything about poverty.
And nothing about the Communist Manifesto.

Or, Mr Tsetung.

They had embraced the red of the revolution.
A colourful antidote to the dull grey of deprivation.

The distance from the railway station to the house,
where she finally got employed, hadn't been easy.

She had to traffic herself:

Sex for food.
Sex for shelter.
Sex for survival.

It was a miracle she had not ended in the red-light quarters of a B-grade town.

Her employer was a Punjabi man –
A widower and a *dhaba* owner;

With a daughter of eight.

It wasn't easy for Maya there, too.
But the miseries were bearable;
Within the walls.
And not on the streets.

It was still a sanctuary,
With just one man to ravage her.

And occasionally, his friends.

Bearable.
Bearable.
Oh god, so bearable.

Because it came with perks:
Sleep, food and shelter.

The bearable asylum of domesticity.

There were things,

Piling up on her head,
Just like prosaic everyday objects –
In a typical home.

Parents hacked by rebels.
Chastity surrendered.
Rape, repeated ad nauseam.
Gun at nine.
Killing government soldiers.
Living in camps.
Romantic escapades.
Raids.
Flight, hunger and then migration to India.
Its mean streets.
The embrace of strange men.
Survival in the city.

A list of revolution and its aftermath.

She'd think all this
And heave,
Or try to.

Constantly
Feeling stifled,
With no sign of second wind.

Or, a wee bit of silence.

Rolling in her bed.
Roiling in her head.

Tossing.
Turning.

And trying.

Very hard to *undo* things.

To *rewrite* history.

Until, the darkness in her room,
The fraught silence.

Would be broken –

By a hiss,

Coca-Cola.

58, 59

Whatnot

Chibo.

It's a derelict village,
In the *fabled* Darjeeling.

The journey starts here.

Of Ruben.

He is at the Kalimpong syndicate.
It's the only taxi stand in town.

10 kilometres from Chibo.

Ruben is running away from home.

He is just 14,
In school.

And an orphan.

His uncle brought him up.

A peon at the post-office.
A mean man, rustic is his meanness.

He feeds Ruben with pig food
And makes him sleep in the sty.

It is *horrific*.

The nearest city is Siliguri.
A two-hour drive from Kalimpong.

He has no clue where he is headed.
But he has chosen to make *nowhere* home.

The only other place he has heard of is Mumbai, on the radio.

The city of dreams –
Superstars *and* Bollywood.

Its lure is too strong to resist.

In fact, *anything* can lure *anyone* from Kalimpong.
After the Gorkha uprising (for the identity of the Indian –Nepalese).

After years of tumult
And terror.

After 1,200 deaths.

After nothing.

At noon, he reaches Siliguri.
And then heads off to the railway station.

It's his first time at a station.

He steps into a train,
With Bollywood in his head.

After thirty-six hours, he is here.
At the la-la land.

But.

He mixes up the cities.
And lands up in Delhi instead.

This doesn't stop him –
From dreaming.

He decides to make some money.
And then travel to Mumbai.

At first, he aims for the good life.
He looks for jobs in Jorbagh.

None employ him.

One, he is a juvenile.
Two, he is a Nepali.

Born in India.
An Indian citizen.

But.

No one wants to understand the difference.

He has been labelled –
Not worthy of trust.

This takes him back to Old Delhi,
Towards the railway station.

There, a *chowmein* shop owner,
An Oriya,
Employs him.

For a pittance.

He takes it,
Without any questions asked.
He has at least got a roof above him now.

It's the kitchen of the moveable van.
The *Chowmein* Shop.

The other employees are all Nepalese from Nepal.
And homosexuals.

Who love making out at night –
In this wretched van –
In the Delhi heat.

In this sweaty dystopia.

After a year, Ruben is drained.
But he has learned the ways of life.

The hard way.

The place where he delivers chowmein regularly is a tyre-repair shop.
The owner is an old Punjabi uncle.
He is both kind and giving.

He teaches him a life-skill –
To fix tyres.

Eventually, to hire him.

Things change for the better.

Just like those tyres.

By now, Ruben is not Ruben,
Everyone calls him *Bahadur*.

Bahadur means brave.
But when Nepalese are called by that name, it means something else.

A pejorative like *nigger*.

At the Punjabi man's house, he meets Maya.

Maya works there.
She is from Nepal.

It doesn't take time
For them to exchange glances –
And then to elope.

In search of a better life.

Nowhere.

Thankfully, they have some money saved.

They buy a *mucktoo* from INA market.
And a second-hand table from Lajpat.
And open a roadside *momos* shop.

Delhi-*wallahs* love momos.
Their business swells.

One night, they do it –

With sweet abandon.

And soon,
Maya is pregnant.

It comes to them as a bittersweet news.

They have money,
But not so much.

The realization dawns on them,
After they visit a doctor.

Things worsen.

It's a complicated pregnancy.

Ruben tries all sorts of options.
Driver. Watchman. Cook.
Nothing works out.

Until now,
They were living in a night shelter.
But soon, they'll have to move into a flat.

At least, a 1 BHK,
In a decent area.

The horrors of which terrify the two.
No one lets out flats to bahadurs.

After several attempts,
They find one.

The ritual of convincing and offering an extra 5000/- clinches the deal for them.

'Okay.
We'll take it,'
They say.

Their expenses soar.

Ruben goes loco,
With the surging pressure.

He starts visiting brothels,
To get some load off his head.

There, he learns about gigolos.

Also, the fact that men like him only get to please the crooks.
Or the policemen.

But not the ladies.

This career of his –
Begins with blowjobs.

Hand-jobs.
Sodomy.
And whatnot.

But, his income increases steadily.
Maya is in no state to ask him all of that.
As long as the cash is flowing in.

On special occasions,
Especially on the bachelor's night of lowlifes,
He gets to earn extra.

It's a package deal.

He has to roam the streets of Delhi –
With a group of men in a car;
Pleasing them as much as possible.

Oh hell.

By now, he has begun enjoying it.
As if to say, he has come to terms
With his alternative sexuality.

As the pregnancy advances.
The money is never enough.
He *has* to make *more*.

His colleagues from the street have an advice for him,
'Change your sex.
Trans are in demand.'

'You'll make more.'

Maya has no option but to agree to it.

It's a fucked-up situation.

A doctor asks Ruben for seven lakh.
For the sex-change procedure.
He is the cheapest one.

Ruben turns to his pimp.
He *says,* 'There's no free lunch on the streets.

But there is always a job.

It's a quick one,'
His pimp tells him.

It's a property feud case.
Nephew wants his uncle murdered.
The uncle is a dirty old moneylender.

Ruben signs up for it.
He plans the murder.
For months.

Dexterously.

There's no margin for error;
Only a chance.

The grand puja
At Chawri Bazaar.

The old moneylender
Steps out *only* then.

In broad daylight
And in the midst of a throng.
Ruben murders him.

Nine jabs with a screwdriver.
All over the moneylender's body –

Including his eyes.
He gets the money.
But he can't stay in the city.
The heat is on.

It has made the headlines.

He takes refuge in his pimp's village –
In the Arra District of Bihar.
A breeding ground for criminals.

A *pestilential well.*

After six months of laying low.
His love for Maya takes him back to Delhi.

He arrives in the dead of the night.
But doesn't visit Maya.
He fears that the police might be keeping a watch.

The sex-change becomes his only option –
To hide from the eyes of the law.

He prepares himself,
Keeping his child in his mind.

He does it.
Eventually.
And turns into a woman.

When he has recovered from the procedure.
He feels like visiting Maya.
Again.

On the way, he meets his pimp,
Who fails to recognize him.

Ruben is *different* now.

Although, it is only through him he is sending her the money.

The pimp doesn't have good news for him.

It's not the baby.
It's not the crime.
It's not Maya.

All of that is fine.

In fact, the Sardarji at the tyre shop has given Maya and his baby refuge.

'But why can't I meet them?'
Ruben asks the pimp.

The pimp hands him a letter.
It's from Maya.

The content of it is long and winding.
Word after *word.*
That mean nothing to him now.

Except one bit.

For now, let's just suffice it by saying:

It was about 200 *rupees,*
To buy the *mucktoo.*

72, 73

Idol worship

Imagine an island.
Imagine getting stuck there.
Imagine not having a way out.
Imagine being told: you don't belong there.

Where do you go?
What do you do?

Crippling.
Isn't it?

That's Darjeeling.
That's the fate of the Indian Nepalese there.
That's their plight, their reality and their identity.

They're neither Indian, nor Nepalese.

It is like having the air to breathe but not having the right to do so.

Asphyxiating –
Would be the word.

The history of their quest for identity is a long and tumultuous one.
But that's not the story for today.

The story is about heroes.
Or more precisely, the lack of it.

A brief background on heroes and the economy of identity politics warrants a space here.
Darjeeling has been a victim of such political dynamics.

For years, in fact more than a hundred years, every political banner has rallied on and made a killing on the topic branded as 'Gorkhas'.

How they've contributed to the nation –
At the line of control with Pakistan;
At wars.

As if the Indian–Nepalese are capable of nothing more than being fodder to godforsaken wars.

Albeit, the rhetoric never seems to lose steam among the locals there.
Quite like the fabled Darjeeling toy train.

However, since 2008, the dialogue has changed.
The Internet revolution has made people more informed.
And opinionated.

The zeitgeist is a mixed feeling.
There is a political vacuum,
Fallow with opportunities.

In a little shanty in Darjeeling, a family is watching *National Idol*.
Among the many contestants, a Nepalese, too, is there.
It is unclear, thus far though, whether he is from India or Nepal.

As if it mattered.

Jim's progress is swift.

The judges adore him.
The fans simply love him.
His appeal is spreading like wildfire –
In Kolkata, Mumbai and now also Delhi.
He's conquered them all.

Boom!

Finally, they get to know who he really is.
A short film advertises the fact that he is a policeman stationed in a barrack in Kolkata.

The Nepali-speaking people around the world go crazy.

Overnight, he is a star.

Although, he *hasn't* won the *National Idol* yet.

For that, he has to win the votes.
Votes sent by fans through text messages.

40 million Nepalese—their imagination fired—go berserk.

It is reported that busloads cross the border at Kakarvitta,
Just to buy an Indian SIM to vote.

Such is the intensity and scale.

Women's self-help groups,
Gorkha Rifle Retired Club,
The Drivers' Youth Society,
The village Panchayat,

All come together to vote.

Funds are set up.

The vegetable vendor sells his produce to vote.
The cobbler fixes a shoe to vote.
The beggar collects alms to vote.
Even the village fool sells his father's goat to vote.

Soon, it's a movement –
On a scale never seen before –
Something has to give.

Someone sees something more in that organized chaos,
the frenzy to elect an idol.
An opportunity to topple the status quo and it
happens, he wins.

The ruling party, initially ambivalent in its support for this new hero, finds the ground moving from under its feet.

The old order is changing.

It's not a musical show anymore.

It's a revolution.

Or that's what the political protagonists think,
As they create a new party.

With its baggage of issues, symbols, myths and action plans.

Jim, in the meanwhile, slips back into the anonymity of his policeman's uniform.

Once their purpose is served.

Forgotten except on the Internet.
Cached and archived in stale news pages of
days gone by.

Mentioned in essays by dim-witted academics, too
slow to comprehend and anticipate the phenomenon he
created with his musical pretensions.

Pretty as fuck

Sam had just joined a design firm,
After a year on sabbatical.

Resuscitated and resurrected –
From the burnout at the butt-end of a decade's work.

He'd got this new job through an influential recommendation.
A designation he took great pride in.

He had a team under him.
Reputed clients and lucrative portfolios.

It was a power trip all the way.

But corporate success comes with a price,
And in his case, it was his family life.

There was a crisis in the offing.
His decade-long relationship was at breaking point.

At such a juncture, he received a text on Facebook.
It was from a girl, *pretty as fuck*.

Initially, he thought it was a mistake –
Perhaps someone looking for a job.

But later, he realized the request was genuine.

Designers were of particular interest to her.
She thought they knew the value of beauty.

She'd taken a liking to Sam's art on Facebook.

Beautiful, visually appealing posts,
Minimally designed – modern and majestic.

After that, Sam got busy with routine,
Got in the thick of things at the firm.

Then.

While at a meeting, he received another message on Facebook.

It was a YouTube link.
The song was: 'Please like me like you want to'
By Ben Harper and Jack Johnson.

The song was his favourite of late.
For, he hadn't been able to understand the resigned nature of his girlfriend of years.
Sam responded with a simple, 'Hello!'

And thus, began their online romance.

His messages were maniacal,
Bursting with bravado.

When deep inside, it was a cry for help.

The girl hardly spoke.
She just sent him links of beautiful songs.

Until this point, he'd just known a few things about her.

The fact that she was in college,
Half as young as he was,

And that she was in Athens.

If it were to his whims, he'd have called her up first thing –
On Facebook.

She hadn't given him her phone number yet.

Also, there was the problem of time difference,
Between Delhi and Athens.

And he'd have to wait till midday.

She temped as a receptionist in an Art Gallery.
Otherwise, she was in college.

The fact that she worked at an art gallery clicked.
Sam had found someone who he could talk to at length about art.

After two hours, the girl would yawn.
And request Sam to go to sleep.

She was strange.

Sam had been in a long-distance relationship before.
And he understood the problem of isolation in foreign countries.

On days when Sam got busy, she kept texting him on Facebook. And he would skip meetings and work, just to respond to her.

Initially, it was texts and voice calls.
But soon they were seeing each other – online.

She showed him her pretty toes.
And he the world to her.

The girl was pretty as fuck,
And Sam fantasized about her and began dissipating.

He was obsessed with her.
He craved for that daily fix of her voice.

Even though his girlfriend was there at his home.

The girl enticed him with provocative pictures.
And Sam began planning a secret trip to Athens.

The exchanges became frequent and suddenly they seemed to have so many things in common.

Like both of them belonged to political families.

So their talk digressed beyond the romantic pleasantries to weightier matters like the state of the country.

Such exchanges only fuelled their desire to be together.

The countdown for her arrival began.
The waiting became unbearable for him.

A week before the Delhi elections, she landed.
She declined Sam's offer to pick her up.

But their interactions on social media continued.

Sam's obsession with her showed no signs of abating.
He wanted to end his present relationship to be with her.

But before that, he wanted to meet her face to face –
After all, physical proximity was important.

Even necessary for the kind of future he was planning with her.

She agreed, finally.

Then the unspeakable happened –
She revealed herself to him on a WhatsApp video call.

What followed was disturbing.

She was a middle-aged cripple,
On a wheelchair.

The Facebook profile was that of her dead daughter.

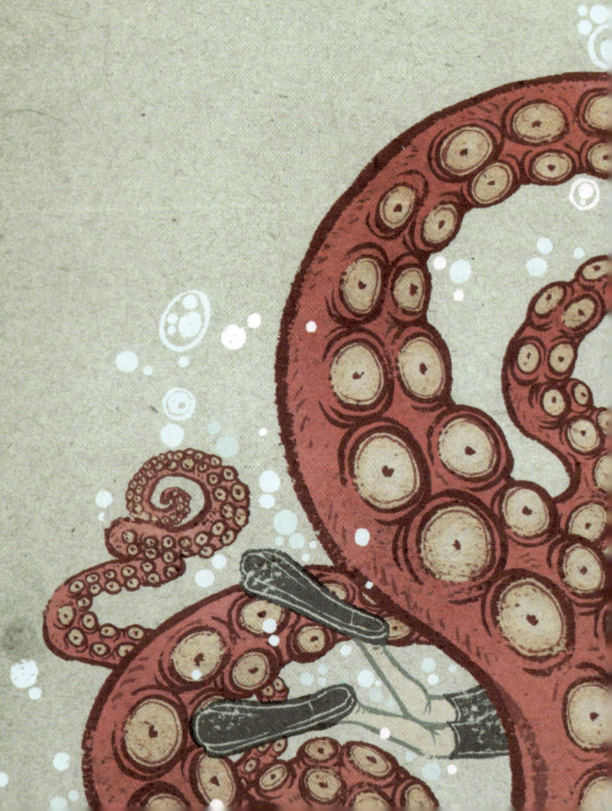

Object Lesson

Bin.

A trash bin.

Yes, it begins here.

The detritus of domesticity,
Used sanitary napkins, pieces of fruit,
Rats darting along a maze of egg trays.

He has a vague recollection of the previous night.

A trip to the chemist shop,
A jab of ketamine.

Ketamine.
His purchase of silence.

Otherwise, life is not worth it.

At the ripe age of twenty one, he has seen it all:
Alcoholism, separation, unemployment.

Coursing through the interstices of Darjeeling.
Looking for the next fix.

It's a dull day, fogged up.

Suddenly, a car stops in front of him.

They bundle him inside and put him up for
rehabilitation.

The correction home is hell.

But he is pronounced cured in the end.

A year later

Ruben is clean.
Sprightly.
But deadpan as he goes through the motions of life.
Tracked by a counsellor, whose good-natured
persistence wearies him.

Thoroughly.

After three months of this cat-and-mouse game, he
decides to take charge of his life;
And heads off to Delhi.

To work at a call centre.

The late hours, the easy availability of money and
vodka, takc him on a different trip.

His tolerance for vodka goes beyond a bottle a night.

He tries to take the edge off with music.

He can make magic with his guitar.

Soon, he is playing gigs in the bars.

The money follows;
And fans as well.

He gives up the call centre job to pursue music full-time.
One night, he has a new admirer of his music –
The principal of a reputed school.

Ruben really impresses her.

They meet often.
And despite her marriage, they start seeing each other.

The sex is mind-blowing –
Forbidden sex.

On one such occassion, during a post-coital smoke, she offers him a job.

He takes it up,
As a music teacher at the reputed school.

From there on, he is known as Sir Ruben.

A music teacher in a school, he is a rock star with his flings and his affairs.

He is living life in the fast lane –
Where burnout is inevitable.

And here it comes –

He is fired without notice for his profligate ways.
Actually, petty jealousy does him in.

Jealousy between the principal and a junior teacher.

He survives for a while,

On meagre savings and playing at seedy bars.
But opportunities dry up.

The place is infested with musicians and it is time for him to pack up and move.

Back in Darjeeling, he tries all sorts of jobs.
And finally settles, to join a new political outfit.

Not out of any idealism.

He is merely following the money.

But it's not cushy, as he had imagined it to be.

His party is new.
It's jostling for space.

Turf wars are inevitable.

The old will give way to the new, but not so easily.

Then one evening . . .

The cadres of the rival party waylay him.
Beat him up on the street.

And knock him down back into the bin.

Lost in Transcription

M was a child of much promise.
He was the star of the Roy family.

He could recite *The Charge of the Light Brigade*.
Verbatim, flawless and fast.

It was a record, both at home and school.

> 'Half a league, half a league,
> Half a league onward,
> All in the valley of Death
> Rode the six hundred.'

But morning doesn't show the day.

M failed in class 10.
Science *fucked* him up.

Seeing a clear lack of opportunity in his small town, M decided to move to Bengaluru.

In search of a job.

With his qualifications, he didn't have much choice.
It was either a call centre or subtitling firm.

He chose the latter.

The money was less.
But it gave him bragging rights back home about his exotic vocation.

Training over, he excelled in his job.
Subtitling, he felt, was in his blood.

He rose through the ranks –
From regional language movies to Bollywood blockbusters.

It was not always easy.

Negotiating the venality of his colleagues –
The backstabbing and bitching.

His aim then turned into becoming one among the big boys.
Hollywood movie subtitlers were at the *top* of the food chain.

That was the ultimate thing.

But there were many things to negotiate through.

English major graduates.
Subtitling veterans.
The boss's pets.
The tireless sycophants and their unceasing small-talks.

The list didn't end there.

There were other formidable challenges.

Managing everyday affairs,
Upgrading his skills,
Diploma in foreign languages – French/Spanish.

And to make matters worse, he got romantically involved with a colleague.

C, a trainee.

But then.

Life *is* full of surprises.

One fine day, one of the big boys *fucked up*.
He couldn't deliver the subtitling of *The Lord of the Wings*.

The brief was opened to everyone in the firm.

This, definitely, was an opportunity for M –
And for everyone else.

There was a mad scramble for the job;
Colleagues vied with each other to please the bosses.

M was confident as usual –
As he was the most well-read, if not the most qualified.

He had already read the book twice.

On the day of internal presentation, M stole the thunder.

The management apprised everyone about the result being announced a day after.

The clockwork of internal politics went berserk.
Private lunches, special favours, on-the-sly texts, you name it.

M cared less.

For, if not the project, he had the job.
And C.

That evening went on as usual.

M and C had dinner and sex.
And a dreamless, peaceful sleep after that.

In the morning, the day brimmed with possibilities.

Everyone was on time at work.

A meeting was called to declare the chosen candidate for the prized project.

It was quite confusing.
Cryptic, too.

M's subtitles were chosen.

But.

The much-qualified C would be the face of the project.

The film franchise wanted a good profile is what they said.

It was bittersweet for M.
But he said, fuck it.

That way, everything got resolved,
Just in a typical corporate manner.

The project got approved by the client.

And the subtitling company celebrated the success of it.

Later, at the Indian premiere of the blockbuster, the movie ended, the credits scrolled.

And there in the dim lights of the multiplex M and C lingered.

Only to find that it wasn't M or C.

Or even M & C.

They had replaced it with the name of the Subtitling Company.

The end.

Sometimes I think the purpose of life is to reconcile us to its eventual loss by wearing us down, by proving, however long it takes, that life isn't all it's cracked up to be.

— Julian Barnes, *The Sense of an Ending*

ACKNOWLEDGEMENTS

Profound thanks to my wife, Prerna –
for being patient for ten long years.

As if I was up to something great.

To my friend, Riazat Ullah Khan –
for listening to me for the *first* five years.

To my other friend, Suman Adhikary –
for listening to me for the *next* five years.

And then no more.

To my brother, Ashis Panday –
for reading all the edits.

To my teacher, Prabin Moktan –
for editing all the edits.

To my agent, Dipti Patel –
for believing in all the edits.

To my editor, Avneet Kaur –
for making sense of all the edits.

Until the edits turned into a book.

To my art partner, Nidhin Kundathil –
for blindly following me in all my *rackets*.

To my mentor, Jossy Raphael –
for telling me, 'you're either a fool or
a genius'.

To my guardian angel, Yuko Shimizu –
for all the love and kindness.

I couldn't have come *thus far*
without them.

To my father, Kishan Panday –
for getting me *acclaim* in my town.

To my late mother, Winnifred Panday –
for being my *raison d'être*.

And to Dr Shashi Tharoor –
for never ceasing to inspire and
support me.

I'm *indebted* to all of them to the point
of *almost* bankruptcy.